The King's Secret

PATRICIA FORDE

Illustrated by

Donald Teskey

THE O'BRIEN PRESS
DUBLIN

First published 1993 by The O'Brien Press Ltd.,
20 Victoria Road, Dublin 6

2 3 4 5 6 7 8 9 10
95 96 97 98 99 00 01

British Library Cataloguing-in-publication Data
Forde, Patricia
Lowry Lynch
I. Title II. Teskey, Donald
823.914 [J]

The O'Brien Press receives assistance from
the Arts Council/An Chomhairle Ealaíon.

ISBN 0-86278-340-2

Typesetting, layout and design: The O'Brien Press
Cover illustration: Donald Teskey
Cover design: The O'Brien Press
Cover separations: Lithoset, Dublin
Printing: Cox & Wyman Ltd., Reading

The King's Secret

Patricia Forde

Director of the Galway Arts Festival, Patricia was a primary school teacher for seven years. She also writes for television and has worked with Macnas, Galway's innovative street theatre group, for whom her book *Tír Faoi Thoinn* was first written as a script. She studied Old Irish at Galway University, and has a particular interest in mythology and folklore.

THE PUBLISHERS
would like to remind
readers that *Queenie*
and *Bridie* are two
unusually dreadful
specimens of mothers
and (thankfully) bear no
resemblance to any
persons living or dead.
Lowry, Seamus and all
the others, of course, are totally true-to-life, and may
remind you of someone you know. But don't tell
them or you'll never hear the end of it!

DEDICATION

For Josie, with all my love

When our great, great, great, great, great, great grandparents were only knee high to a grasshopper, a king ruled all of

Ireland. His name was Lowry.
Lowry Lynch.

Now, Lowry lived with his
mother, Queenie, in a large
castle at the top of a hill.
Lowry's mother was very proud
of him and thought he was a
very good king.

He always tidied his room. He
never gave back-answers. He
was a lot better about going to
bed on time than most kings his
age. And he always smiled
politely when his Aunt Molly
insisted on kissing him.

In fact, Queenie only ever had one problem with Lowry. His hair!

Lowry would not have his hair cut and he wore it long and wild. It flowed down his back,

and gathered in curls round his
ankles! It fell in the soup, it
blocked up the sink – and it was
a full-time job to keep the birds
from making their nests in it.
Very small children would
sometimes get caught up in it
and disappear for days at a time!

As if that were not bad
enough, Lowry also wore a hat.
An ugly, battered hat, not a bit
kingly. Day in, day out, he wore
that hat, whatever the weather.
It was too much for any mother.

So, when you think about it, it

was no wonder that Queenie
and Lowry had many a good
row. The villagers of that time

would tell you how they were
kept awake at night because of
the fighting at the castle.

'You will go to the barber
tomorrow!' Queenie would
screech.

'No, Mammy, I won't! I won't,'
Lowry would yell.

'You'll go if I have to drag you
there by the hair of your big fat
head!' Queenie would shout.

The villagers didn't mind being
kept awake really, because it
was good fun to listen to and
there never was much on TV in

those days. In fact there was *no*
TV in those days, so what else
did they have to amuse
themselves?

Finally, at the end of her tether, Queenie came up with a solution.

'Son,' she announced, 'I'll stop going on about this hair business, though God knows I'll never understand it, if –' and here she paused and looked her son straight in the eye . . .

'If, Mammy?' prompted Lowry timidly.

'If you agree to get a haircut once a year on the first day of spring,' she said quickly. She stopped to catch her breath. 'Say you will, son, and I'll make the appointment straight away.'

'No, Mammy!' said Lowry firmly and he tossed his heavy golden locks back over his shoulder. 'I will *not* get my hair cut and that's that!'

'That's it then!' screamed his mother. 'I've had it with you! You're grounded, impounded and I'll see to it that you're HOUNDED, until you agree with my plan.'

Poor Lowry! He was shaking in his boots. He knew he would

not get a minute's rest until he
gave in. His mother was as
stubborn as a mule.

'All right so,'
he sighed. 'I
agree!

But on one condition.'

'What? What condition?' roared his mother. 'It had better be good! I warn you.'

'I will agree,' said Lowry slowly, 'to having my hair cut once a year on the first day of spring, if –'

'What? If what?' bellowed his mother, jumping up and down with rage.

Lowry took a deep breath. He gathered all his courage together and spoke calmly and firmly.

'I will agree,' he said, 'if the

barber be executed, murdered, head chopped off – the works – as soon as the job is done!' He folded his arms and waited.

Queenie smiled fondly at him.

'Is that what all this is about?'
she purred. 'My little Lowry
doesn't like barbers? Why, that's
no problem, my little pumpkin!'
and she tweaked Lowry's
chubby cheek.

'We'll have them toasted,
roasted, grilled, barbecued or
fried if you'll just get that hair
cut!' Her voice rose a tone at the
end.

Now, if Queenie had been
brighter she might have noticed
that Lowry still wasn't too happy
and that he pulled his large,

floppy hat down over his face more than ever. But Queenie wasn't bright, and she didn't notice – so let's not waste any more time on that!

Well! That day marked the end of the peaceful lives of the people in the village. No longer did they lean out of their windows of an evening to hear the royal battles. Oh no! A much more exciting entertainment had come to town. The LOTTERY!

Yes, my friends, in this small village all those years ago the first ever GRAND LOTTERY was held. And the winner? The winner would cut the King's hair!

Great, eh? Especially when you consider that whoever cut the King's hair got put to death! Think about it.

But how else could they decide who would do the job? You couldn't very well put an ad in the paper, now could you? So, the villagers invented the LOTTERY. They would spin the wheel of fortune and the person whose name came up would get the scissors. Well, people lived in fear of the first day of spring.

On that day, the villagers gathered in the main square to watch the wheel being spun.

It was a great day out for all the family. The square was full of hawkers of all sorts from early morning.

They sold hamburgers, ice-cream, souvenir scissors, fantastic hair sculptures made of gold and silver, miniature lottery wheels, locks of hair of all colours in little boxes made from

cow's horn – almost anything you could ever want.

Over in one corner of the square there was a gang taking bets on the outcome. Lowry and Queenie attended and spent the morning talking and joking with the villagers.

The main attraction was, of course, Jack Spinner, who had got the job of spinning the wheel. On the dot of twelve o'clock he strolled up to the wheel to start the show.

'Roll up! Roll up!' Jack yelled,

trying to catch the attention of
the crowd.

'Lovely diction,' old ladies
sighed to each other.

'Ladies and gentlemen!' Jack
continued. 'We are gathered
here today for the greatest event
of the year! The high point of

the social season
– the LOTTERY!

Who will it be, my friends? What
poor unfortunate will have to

cut the King's hair? Roll up! Roll up! Watch the names as they fly by! Will it be you, or will it be me? Only the wheel can tell!'

And with that, he gave the wheel an almighty spin and the game was on. Some people thought Jack was a bit over the top, but as Jack himself said, 'That's showbiz!'

Everyone was trembling, waiting to see who would win the LOTTERY.

There was a young man in the village called Seamus and he

lived with his widowed mother, Bridie, in a little house near the square. Bridie's greatest wish was that her son should be a doctor. Then the neighbours would see that they were as posh as anyone.

The boy didn't like the idea at all. *He* wanted to be an astronaut or an actor or a ringmaster in a circus. Something exciting. But he went along with her in order to keep the peace – and he spent all day reading books about exciting

lives and writing long poems
that never rhymed about
running away to sea and training
lions to jump through hoops.

'Always buried in a book! Why
can't you do something
normal?' his mother would
mutter a hundred times a day.

But Seamus and his mother did
have one thing in common.
They did *not* want him to
become the King's barber. They
watched the LOTTERY in fear
and trepidation.

'Oh, please God it won't be

you, Seamus. Useless and all as
you are, I wouldn't give that
Queenie one the satisfaction and
let you cut that lad's hair!' the
Widow said. 'Jumped up! That's
what those two are! I knew them

when they had nothing!'

At twelve o'clock, the wheel was spun and Seamus and his mother watched it closely. With their eyes glued to his name, their heads went round and round with the wheel, getting slower and slower and slower as it came to a stop. His name was moving towards the top! With one last click, the giant wheel stopped . . . and the name at the top was . . . Seamus, the Widow's son!

'And it's . . . Seamus!'

announced Jack Spinner, as mothers and sons all over the square fainted with relief, and little girls took their chance and grabbed half-eaten ice-creams out of their hands.

'Ah! Ohh! Ugh!' screamed Bridie, as she raced off home to hide her shame. 'We're ruined! Ruined! The thought of you having to cut that young pup's hair! You, that I was going to make a doctor out of! Now a common barber! What will the neighbours say? Oh, I can't face

it! The disgrace! What will we
do? What will we do? WHAT WILL
WE DO?' and she all but fell in a
dead faint at the thought of it.

'Mother!' said Seamus. 'It's all
right. You won't have to worry

about the neighbours.
Remember, when the job is
done I'll be put to death!'

'Mmm!' said his mother,
calming down a little and
looking up from where she lay
sprawled on the floor. 'I
suppose they couldn't call you
Seamus the Barber after you
only doing the one job, could
they?'

'Still, they'll hardly call you
Seamus the Doctor either,' she
added bitterly.

'There's nothing for it,'

announced the Widow, finally. 'I'll have to crawl on my hands and knees to that oul' hag, Queenie, and ask her to spare your life.'

'Whatever you think, Mother,' answered the boy in his usual bored voice.

But his mother had not quite finished. 'To think of all I do for you,' she wailed. 'And what do I get in return? What indeed! A useless article the like of you, can't turn a sod or milk a cow! A lad that's only fit for turnin' pages and sayin' oul' poems that would make a person queer in the head.'

On and on like this she went all the way to the palace with Seamus tagging along behind, wishing he had a walkman so that he wouldn't have to listen – but they hadn't been invented yet, so he just had to put up with it. He put his fingers in his ears instead. Well, it was better than nothing.

At last they reached the castle and Seamus's mother knocked

on the big oak door.
The butler
opened it and
stared at them
for a moment.

'Ah – this is the barber, I presume?' he said in his posh palace voice.

'No,' the widow replied calmly. 'This is my son, the soon-to-be-doctor, as it happens. Now, go and fetch old Queenie instead of standing there gawking!'

When the butler saw the blazing look in the Widow's eye he ran as fast as he could to fetch Lowry's mother.

'Well, Queenie, isn't it grand you're looking,' said the Widow sweetly when she finally appeared.

'Ah . . . em . . . em . . . Bridie! So charming to see you again after all these years,' gushed Queenie. 'I see you've brought Seamus the Barber with you! Lowry will be pleased!'

'Yes, well,' said Bridie, 'well, actually, that's what I've come to see you about. I want to . . . to . . . well, actually . . . I want to . . . to plead for his life.'

'You want to *plead* did you say?' laughed Queenie,

delighted. 'Oh, do go ahead, I *love* to hear people plead!'

I'd especially like to hear *you* at it, she thought, but she decided to be polite so she didn't say that. Instead, she flopped down on the steps of the palace to listen to the widow's plea.

Seamus thought his mother would burst with temper. She swallowed hard. Her face turned puce. She opened and closed her mouth several times.

'All right then,' she said at last. 'I'll say what I have to say. If you free my son I will give you my award-winning recipe for Turnip Jam!'

Now the Widow's Turnip Jam was the talk of four counties. Every year it won all the prizes going at the big fair held in the village. It won the prize for the fruitiest, the prize for the sweetest, the prize for the juiciest, and the prize for the chewiest! Queenie, it must be said, won almost every other prize (as was only right and proper – she was, after all, the King's mother) but she could never best the Widow when it came to Turnip Jam.

A long and heavy silence fell. The Widow waited.

Seamus said his longest poem

to himself in his head.

At last, Queenie rose and said:
'Very well. I will speak to my
son!' And off she went, leaving
the Widow to cry bitter tears
over the loss of her one claim to
fame.

'Lowry, dear,' Queenie began,
when she finally found her son
perched on the throne. 'Lowry,
my sweet, would you do your
old mother a favour?'

'Yes, Mumsie, if I can I
certainly will,' replied her
obedient son with a smile.

She came straight to the point. 'Let's not kill the barber today, eh? It's very important to silly old Mumsie that he live. All rightie?' And her eyes glazed over as she thought of the prizes that would soon be hers.

'But . . . but you promised!' sobbed the King, big tears rolling down his chubby cheeks.

'Now, just stop that!' yelled Queenie, with a sudden change of mood. 'It's the one and only time I've ever asked you for a special favour, you wretch!'

'But . . . but . . .' blubbered her
son. 'But then everyone will
know my secret!'

'Secret?' roared his mother. 'What secret? You never said anything to me about a secret! A boy should never have secrets from his mother! What's this secret that you're so worried about?' and with a piercing shriek she caught Lowry by his hair and shook him until his teeth chattered.

Just then the butler came in to tell Queenie that the Widow was reconsidering her kind offer due to the fact that she had been kept waiting so long.

'All right then, dear?' said Queenie sweetly to her son (she would never let herself down in front of the servants). 'We can talk about this later!'

Lowry was trying hard to catch his breath.

'For the moment, though, we won't kill the barber and he won't tell your secret! Okay? Then we can all be happy!'

'All right so,' choked Lowry through his tears. 'Show him in.'

And so it came to pass that Seamus the Widow's son cut the

King's hair and in doing so
discovered the King's secret.
'Horse's ears!' screeched

Seamus in shock and horror.
'You have the ears of a horse!'

'Will you stop with your roaring!' said poor Lowry anxiously. 'You don't have to let everyone know. Yes, I have horse's ears. An old witch put a spell on me years ago. If my mother found out she'd kill me!'

'Why's that?' asked Seamus, full of curiosity now.

'Well, everyone knows that a king who has horse's ears would be fired. I'd be out on my . . . Well, anyway, it's very important to my mother that her son is king. What would the neighbours say if we had to go back to being boring and ordinary like you? My mother would never let me hear the end of it.'

'I know what you mean,' said Seamus, thinking of his own mother.

'And,' said the King, making a clean breast of it all, 'that's why I always wear a hat and that's why I wear my hair long and that's why I want my barber to die. But remember *you've* promised never to tell my secret to a single soul!'

Now, poor Seamus was dying to tell someone there and then, but he went straight home without speaking to anyone at all.

What a time he got from his mother though.

'A secret? Tell me! Tell me, can't you! After all I've done for you. When I think of me Turnip Jam! You're an ungrateful wretch of a son and no doubt about it!'

She ranted on and on for hours.

But the boy held firm through all the coaxing and threatening. He would not tell the secret. Finally, the Widow gave up.

Seamus soon became ill from keeping the King's awful secret.

He could not eat. He could not sleep. He couldn't read. He couldn't laugh. Over and over again he heard the voice in his head: 'Lowry the King has horse's ears! Lowry the King has horse's ears!'

Finally, his mother could stand it no longer and she sent for the wise woman of the place, Ciara the Clever.

'This boy is keeping a secret,' announced Ciara after much thought.

'Didn't I tell you that already!'

screeched Bridie.

'Well, that's what's making him sick,' said Ciara calmly.

'You see!' screamed the Widow at her son. 'I told you to tell me! But no! *You* knew better! Look where it's got you now!'

'Ciara,' said Seamus, ignoring her. 'I have promised not to tell this secret to a living person and I will keep that promise. But have you no cure for my illness?'

Ciara thought for a long time before answering.

'You will have to go to the forest,' she said finally. 'There you will find a strong willow tree and you must whisper your secret to the tree. Then you will be cured.'

Ciara got up to leave, waiting only for the Widow to go to the jug for her money.

'Money for old rope,' grumbled Bridie as she counted out the gold coins. 'Talking to trees! What next? Oh, 'tis easy to fool an oul' widow woman and her son! Nothing's surer than that.' But she went on like this every time she had to part with money, so nobody paid any attention.

Next morning, Seamus took off for the forest. He found the willow tree and whispered to it: 'Lowry the King has horse's ears!

Lowry the King has horse's ears!'
He said it so quietly that Bridie,
who was hiding behind another

tree, couldn't make out a word he said and she was raging.

Seamus was instantly cured and went home laughing and skipping with a weight gone off his heart. Bridie, on the other hand, hobbled home in her high-heeled shoes which were pinching her, angry and miserable and none the wiser.

Well, that would have been the end of my story but for Harpy Horan. Now, I know it's very late in the story to be introducing you to new people, but it can't be helped.

Harpy Horan was one of Horans the Harpists (no relation to Horans the Butchers or for that matter Horans the Step Dancers or indeed Horans the Yanks, though his family did live very near to Horans the Cat Stealers for a while). Harpy Horan worked at the palace. As you may have guessed, Harpy was a harpist. Actually, Queenie and Lowry hated harp music, but they thought it was very posh to have a royal harpist, so they just had to have one.

Now, Harpy couldn't play the harp anymore than I can, but it didn't matter because Queenie and Lowry were both tone deaf. Harpy, however, had told them that his old harp was worn out from all the playing he did, just in case they'd think he was doing nothing at all.

Anyway, on the very same day that Seamus went to the forest, Harpy went there too. He went in search of wood for a new harp. When he saw the willow tree he decided it was perfect and ordered his servant to chop it down, which the servant did. In no time at all Harpy had a brand new harp made from the old willow tree.

When Queenie saw the new harp – and the bill for the willow tree – she decided right away to have a party to show it off.

'No point in spending a fortune on a new harp if no one sees it now is there?' she said, and ordered the servants to prepare a party for the entire village.

There was so much work to be done to get ready for the palace do! Everything that could be cleaned was cleaned. Everything that could be cooked was cooked, and everyone who could be invited was invited.

There was great excitement in the village on the night of the party as everyone got dressed up in their Sunday best and set off for the palace.

'Such high-falutin' ideas as people get! You'd think Queenie and Lowry were *someone*. I knew those two when they had nothing. Nothing!' said Bridie when she heard about the party, but she decided to go for a look anyway – and of course she too wore her Sunday best.

Seamus brought a book to read in case the party was grossly boring.

The palace was ablaze with lights. Everyone was welcomed and the entertainment began immediately.

People danced and sang and

told funny stories. Seamus
yawned and read his book.

At last Queenie called for
Harpy the Royal Harpist to play

his new and very expensive harp.

'Thank you! Thank you!' said Harpy graciously as he sat down to play. Silence descended on the gathering. But when Harpy's fingers touched the strings no music was heard – no indeed! All that came from the harp was a voice, and this is what it said: 'Lowry the King has horse's ears! Lowry the King has horse's ears!'

There was such a panic! Lowry flew to the harp and jumped up and down on it to try and stop the terrible words.

Queenie also did her best to
cover up. 'Ha ha!' she shrieked.

'A joke! A little joke to keep the party going!' And she hit Harpy a sharp right hook when she thought no-one was looking.

But it did no good. The harp seemed to have a life of its own.

'Lowry the King has horse's ears!' the harp screamed, getting more and more excited.

Suddenly, all eyes turned to Bridie as she stood up and stuck out her chin. Bridie was a woman with a mission. She walked straight up to the King and pulled off his hat. Then she

lifted him off the harp by his
hair. There were the ears, plain
for all to see.

'Ha! You're not half as posh
now are you!' she shrieked with
delight. 'Look at the cut of him!
Look! Let ye all have a good
look!' Mercilessly, she dragged
him around for all to see.

Some people laughed and
teased him, but a lot of people
did not. They thought Bridie was
being a bit mean.

Then a voice broke from the
crowd. 'Stop! Stop that right

now!' It was Seamus.

'Shut up, will you,' ordered his
mother, 'or I'll clatter you!'

But Seamus would not shut up.
He pushed her out of the way
and took poor
Lowry by the
arm.

'Lowry is a fine king!' he said.
'He made a few mistakes, but
everyone does that! I say he
should still be king!'

A big cheer went up at this
because nobody else really
wanted to be king – and the
food was getting cold.

'As for you!' said Seamus to his
mother, 'we're all getting very
tired of your mean ways. You
should just go home!'

That softened Bridie's cough I
can tell you! She crept out of the
palace without another word.

Lowry saw what Seamus had done and took courage from it. He turned to Queenie and looked at her, fair and square between her two eyes.

'You,' he said, 'should go and get a job for yourself instead of trying to be posh all the time!'

The people cheered again at this, so Queenie thought it better to keep her mouth shut for once!

The villagers were pleased. The King's barber would not be executed, and everyone could live happily ever after.

Well . . . except for Bridie. She never got over the business with the Turnip Jam. As for her son becoming a posh doctor, well, that was not to be! Seamus ran away and joined the circus and had a great life.

Meanwhile, up at the palace, Lowry began to think his ears were rather beautiful. He started to wear ribbons on them and then earrings and after a while he had an earring in his nose as well. He was having the time of his life.

All of this nearly drove his
mother mad, of course. She
begged him to grow his hair
long enough again to cover the
awful ears – but he wouldn't!

Lowry had had enough secrets to last him the rest of his days!

Other books from
THE O'BRIEN PRESS

THE LEPRECHAUN WHO WISHED HE WASN'T
Siobhán Parkinson

A tall tale about Laurence, who is tired of being small!

Paperback £3.99

THE FISHFACE FEUD
Martin Waddell

A lively and funny story set in school with Ernie Flack, Fishface and their gangs. More about them in *Rubberneck's Revenge*, also by Martin Waddell, from the O'Brien Press.

Paperback £3.50

RUBBERNECK'S REVENGE
Martin Waddell

Illustrated by Arthur Robins

Ernie Flack and his friends find themselves in Heap Big Trouble when the deputy Head goes on the warpath in this action-packed Dingwell Street School story.

Paperback £3.50

ART, YOU'RE MAGIC
Sam McBratney

Illustrated by Tony Blundell

Art thinks everyone will love him more if he wears a butterfly tie. But all it does is get him into trouble. Still, he saves the day in the end and now he is everyone's favourite.

Paperback £3.50

The WOODLAND FRIENDS series by Don Conroy

THE OWL WHO COULDN'T GIVE A HOOT!
An owl who cannot hoot? The woodland friends try to
solve this strange mystery ...

Paperback £3.99

THE TIGER WHO WAS A ROARING SUCCESS!
A visitor from foreign lands arrives in the woodlands, but
can the friends help him to return home again?

Paperback £3.99

THE HEDGEHOG'S PRICKLY PROBLEM!
Harry Hedgehog joins the circus – and gets into some
sticky situations ...

Paperback £3.99

THE BAT WHO WAS ALL IN A FLAP!
Ever hear of a flying fox? Harry Hedgehog *sees* one, and
throws everyone into confusion ...

Paperback £3.99

THE LOUGH NEAGH MONSTER

Sam McBratney

Illustrated by Donald Teskey

Ever hear of the Lough NEAGH monster? No? That's because he likes to keep very quiet. Until his cousin from Lough Ness arrives to spoil his peace ...

Paperback £3.99

THE LITTLE BLACK SHEEP

Elizabeth Shaw

How the outcast of the flock saves the day.

Paperback £3.99

ORDER FORM

These books are available from your local bookseller. In case of difficulty order direct from THE O'BRIEN PRESS

Please send me the books as marked

I enclose cheque / postal order for £……… (+ 50p P&P per title)

OR please charge my credit card ☐ Access / Mastercard ☐ Visa

Card number ☐☐☐☐ ☐☐☐☐ ☐☐☐☐ ☐☐☐☐

EXPIRY DATE ☐ ☐ ☐ ☐

Name: ....Tel: ....

Address: ....

....

Please send orders to: THE O'BRIEN PRESS, 20 Victoria Road, Dublin 6.
Tel: (Dublin) 4923333 Fax: (Dublin) 4922777